TREASURE
IN THE
MORNING

—

JULIA'S
JOURNAL

TREASURE IN THE MORNING

MORNING

—

JULIA'S JOURNAL

MARY JARRATT

WITH ILLUSTRATIONS BY

SOPHIE L. BROWN

GSP

Treasure in the Morning – Julia's Journal
Mary Jarratt

Published by Greyhound Self-Publishing 2022
Malvern, Worcestershire, United Kingdom.

Printed and bound by Aspect Design
89 Newtown Road, Malvern, Worcs. WR14 1PD
United Kingdom
Tel: 01684 561567
E-mail: allan@aspect-design.net
Website: www.aspect-design.net

Cover Design Copyright © 2022 Aspect Design
Original photograph Copyright © 2022
ISBN 978-1-909219-95-3

CONTENTS

INTRODUCTION

This is the second story of Justin, Titus and Julia. Set in the 4th Century A.D. when the Roman rule of Britain is waning, it takes place a year or so after their rescue of the Roman city known as Camulodunum in early Roman times from a Saxon war horde. (You can read about it in 'Fires in the Night').

It was suggested that I might write a story about the 'Fenwick Treasure', a collection of gold and silver jewellery and coins that was discovered in 2014. I have taken the liberty to add to the actual treasure a child's spoon for the sake of the story and let the treasure be found much earlier than it was in real life. If you want to see the objects that were discovered you can find them in the Colchester Castle Museum.

Another liberty that I have taken is with the likely dates of use of the Roman Circus. The only one so far discovered in Britain, it had probably fallen into disrepair by the time of this story, but chariot racing was a very popular sport in Roman times and it seemed a pity not to include it!

Again, if you would like to see what has been uncovered and preserved of the Circus in Colchester you can visit the Roman Circus Centre which is now in the middle of housing estates on the edge of Colchester. The address is at the back of this book...it is a very interesting site with displays and interpretative pictures, books and models of chariots. You can also find a drink and snacks at the tearoom!

In this sequel Julia discovers a lot about herself as she begins to put childhood behind her and faces some big changes in her life. She finds that she must confront the preconceptions about slavery and relationships that she has, so far, taken for granted.

The story switches between Camulodunum and the countryside in what is now called Essex, named after the East Saxons.

TREASURE IN THE MORNING

MORNING

—

JULIA'S JOURNAL

CHAPTER 1

Poor Alexander has been writing for me all day as I dictated my story and although he's a slave, I think it's time I had pity on him and stopped.

So now I have, and am sitting here with half-closed eyes, seeing through my lashes the slanting rays of golden sun lying across the marble floor of the atrium.

The sunshine tempts me outside.

It is evening and swallows are twittering and swooping across the old garden which lies at the foot of the great wall that surrounds the city. That wall was the beginning of the

adventure which I had last time I visited my aunt, when Justin, who lives next-door-but-one, Titus, my cousin, and I with some help from the Roman Garrison foiled an attempt by an officer to betray the city to the Saxons.

My aunt comes out to chide me for keeping Alexander so long when she needs him elsewhere.

What for, I wonder?

Her husband being dead, and her son, Titus, being somewhat difficult, she relies on Alexander a great deal.

Also I think she likes the way his dark hair curls around his golden-olive cheeks.

When we last visited her I was hardly more than a little girl, but I have done a lot of growing up lately and now I feel as though I am the older one of the two of us.

I notice things, like the way her face eases when she sees Alexander, and how she turns to look after him when he leaves the room.

I don't know whether my mother has seen these things too. Perhaps I'll ask her.

I think, myself, that it is a great shame that he is only a slave and not for marrying. He is the kindest man I have ever met and is the one person to whom Titus pays the slightest heed, except, perhaps for Justin's father, Centurion Marcus.

That brings my thoughts to the real reason for all this writing, most of which is being done by Alexander. So many important things have happened that I would find it too much to write down all our adventures. However, there are some things that are too private to dictate to him. These I write myself in my journal, which is where I try to make sense of my innermost thoughts and feelings.

The idea to keep a journal came from my friend, Hermione,

whose father is the Commander of a fort here, one of the largest and oldest cities in Britannia; the city where I am staying now, visiting my aunt. It used to be the headquarters of the chief tribe of the area, called Trinovantes, before the Romans came and made it their own capital for a while.

Hermione gets the slave who was her brother's tutor, to write down what she does and who she meets day by day.

Before her father was made commander, they lived in a villa not far from my family's farm. We were friends before her father was promoted to be a commander and the family moved to the City.

It was her suggestion that I should keep a journal too.

However, apart from the effort involved in all that writing, nothing much ever happens at home to make it worth all that effort. Nor do I have a scribe there to write it for me.

Any way who wants to read about the barley growing and the sheep bleating?

My home is totally unlike Hermione's, where people are always coming and going. Her mother takes her visiting nearly every day, or shopping to buy jewellery or silks for new clothes, and there always seem to be handsome young centurions arriving to talk with her father!

I should explain that my father is a retired soldier who was given the farm on retirement from the Roman Army- the 'Eagles' as they are called.

He has a wound, that he got fighting the Tribes and so he gets tired very quickly and we live very quietly with a couple of farm slaves, a cook and household slaves.

However, I did make an effort to write an account of my very boring life and brought it with me to my aunt's so that

13

I could record anything special that happened while I was there.

So, here is what I wrote at home...

Chapter 2

Julia Writes

My Private Journal

It is so hard to settle down at home after all the excitement with Justin and Titus although I am glad to see Father again. I think he is getting slower and is sometimes in pain from his wound.

I find myself thinking about Justin quite often, especially when I look at the account he made for me of our adventures last time we met. I have to say that I don't feel the same about my cousin Titus!

I wonder what the boys are doing, apart from lessons of course.

We sometimes wonder whether the Saxons will come here as they did at Camulodunum…I know they sail their boats up even quite small rivers to look for rich pickings from farms and villas like ours.

It is a fearful thought…I don't fancy life as a Saxon slave if I were kidnapped and carried away…

Maybe I would just be killed.

I surprise myself with all this writing…truth to tell, it is my only way of keeping myself from moping… even though I'm afraid that it is very unexciting; a typical week in my journal would be full of nothing much at all.

However, one week at the end of winter, when the weather had been even duller and colder than I could ever remember, when rain swamped the fields and kept us indoors a great deal, I was extremely bored and feeling very, very lonely so I made the effort to record the main happenings of each day, as follows:

First day:

Woken by Nessa, my slave. Wore one of my two stolas. It was wet, so did some practice writing and watched the raindrops dripping off the pots on the terrace.

Second day:

Woken by Nessa. Wore my other stola. It was wet, though the sun made an effort to shine now and again, Mother made me help mend old cushions. Watched the cloud shadows on the downs and played with Gwyn White-Paw, my kitten.

Third day:

Same as yesterday.

Fourth day:

Excitement!!! Mother and I walked in the windy sunshine to see our neighbour and I listened while they talked for hours. And...Gwyn went missing.

Fifth day:

Gwyn returned looking guilty. Where has he been?!
Did some more writing practice and mending.

Sixth day:

More of the same and it rained again. Gwyn was very twitchy.

Seventh day:

Awoke and was dressing, when WE HAD A VISITOR! He was a travelling preacher come to teach the Followers of the Way in our district.

Mother invited him to eat with us and sent Julius one of the household slaves to fetch our neighbours to come and hear his message.

My father wasn't best pleased at the interruption of his peace and quiet, especially since he was inclined to follow the old religion of Mithras. However, when everyone was gathered, he joined us as the visitor, Brother Lukas, explained some of the sayings of the Christus.

I was only half-listening, since Gwyn was busy chasing his tail in the corner and he looked so amusing that I nearly laughed out loud.

Suddenly, I heard the man say that God the Great Father, cared for the little things, like sparrows.

I remembered that only last week, I had found Gwyn on the terrace, playing with a little bird, tossing it up into the air and pouncing on it when it tried to escape. I'd done my best to rescue it, but when I finally managed to get it away from the kitten, it died in my hands.

I was distraught, looking at the sad little bundle of feathers and the shining black eyes, dulling in death. So God cared too?

I was strangely comforted by that.

Brother Lukas went on to say that God cared even more for us and that too was comforting since I was fairly miserable much of the time here on the farm, with no-one of my own age to talk to except Nessa and she was younger than me and only a slave after all.

So apart from the visit of Brother Lukas, that is a typical dull week of my life here on the farm.

I suppose it's only fair to say that there are days, especially in the spring, when the sun is bright and the wind is blowing and the sky is washed-clean blue, when I do feel quite, quite happy.

I fetch Nessa and we walk over the grassy downs. I close my eyes and stretch out my arms as though I were a bird and able to fly away and find whatever it is I dream of.

(My dreams are hard to put into words. I just want to find some sort of meaning to my life, something bigger and more exciting than life here on the farm.)

Little did I know, when I wrote about the visit of Brother Lukas, that only a few moons later, I would be on my way to spend some weeks again with my aunt who lives in the same town as Hermione! AND that I would have had an amazing adventure right here!

I think that God must have heard my unspoken prayers, because a messenger arrived a few days after I had written my sad little journal to say that my aunt would very much like to see her sister (my mother) since they had not met for many months.

My mother who had given me some searching looks of late, said she thought I was in need of a change and should go with her.

So some while later, when the summer work of the farm was

almost done and Mother thought Father could spare us, Mother, Prisca her body-slave, Nessa and I said farewell to Father and the farm and turned our thoughts to city life.

But to continue my account;... in between the dull week I wrote about at home and the visit to my aunt I had An Amazing Adventure!

I suppose I should be glad for all that writing practice at home which was so tiresome at the time, but has turned out to be a good thing since I have such a great event to record now!

I am still astonished that such a thing could happen to me in those days when summer was just a memory and Autumn was beginning to fill the woods with colour.

Because such a lot happened, there is a lot to write, so I (or at least, mostly Alexander) am writing now at my aunt's house, in between spending time with my friend Hermione and playing with Olivia, Justin's little sister who is very cute. Spending time with Justin's family is a welcome relief from my aunt's house. Their house is quiet in a restful sort of way. They all seem to like each other's company and there are no raised voices and slammed doors: in short, they are a family completely different from my aunt's.

In any house that contains Titus, there is always a lot of noise.

I know Titus is fond of his mother, but he always has to question her orders and often refuses to do as she asks.

Consequently, my aunt's house is full of arguments and recriminations. Everyone seems to talk at the top of their voice, even the slaves shout to one another except for Alexander.

It is very conducive to headaches and I know Mother finds it hard to adjust. As for me, I take refuge in the garden among the pear trees and the damson, under which Alexander, being a man of many parts, has made a bench. It is here that he helps me with writing my account. (And Alexander is now writing for me as I dictate to him)...

So to get back to my adventure...

Chapter 3

An Unexpected Encounter

This is what happened:

Gwyn White-paw is now a grown-up cat and often wanders from the farm and I go to look for him, walking and calling along the ancient trackway that skirts our higher fields, as I was doing one mild day at the beginning of Autumn, when there were blackberries to gather.

Gwyn eventually came rustling through the bushes beside the track.

As I bent to pick him up, I heard another rustle, quickly stilled. I spun round, but could see nothing.

I didn't know why, but my heart started to thump unpleasantly and my footsteps quickened.

As I hurried, almost running, along the track to the way down the fields to our villa, I caught a glimpse out of the corner of my eye of something blue among the bushes.

Gwyn objected to being jolted around and struggled free from my arms, landing with a mew of indignation on the ground.

He disappeared into the bushes and I heard a quickly stifled gasp.

I didn't know whether to run and hope Gwyn came home soon or to be brave and stop, maybe call for help, (though I don't think anyone would have heard me) and see who was following me.

As I hesitated, Gwyn reappeared followed by a girl in a

tattered stola which had once been bright blue, I think.

She was dirty, her hair tangled and her feet scratched and bleeding.

She limped out of the bushes.

We stood staring at one another.

My voice came out all croaky as I asked who she was.

She told me her name, Flavia, and then she whispered, "Please help me".

When I said nothing, she began to tell me, in a strange, flat voice with no feeling in it, about the terrible thing that happened to her family when two Saxon war bands came.

The things that she told me are too horrible to write down in full.

In short, the Saxons stole their cattle, set fire to their home and killed the men of the family as they tried to fight.

As I listened to her story, tears began to run down my face, but *she* just went on as though it had happened to someone else.

She and her brother were separated and she doesn't know what happened to her mother and the baby.

Flavia was able to escape and fled, not knowing which direction to take except to put as much distance as possible between her and the Saxons.

She had wandered alone and afraid for four days since then, drinking from streams and eating blackberries.

What else could I do but take her home with me?

I explained it all to my mother who gave the starving girl some food, some water to wash herself in and some clean clothes.

I gave her my yellow stola to wear and we tended the sores on her feet with ointment.

Then my mother took a comb and sat Flavia beside her while she gently teased out the tangles from her long dark hair.

I was surprised that she did this herself instead of getting her body slave or Nessa to do it, but when I saw how Flavia leaned against her and began to lose that frozen look, I understood.

It was several days later, that as she tripped on a loose stone outside and twisted her ankle, she began to cry.

Mother came running and held her tightly and Flavia sobbed and sobbed as though she just couldn't stop.

I sat beside her and stroked her hand for a while, then decided I would do better to get Nessa to fetch some warm milk for Flavia and a cup of wine for mother.

Later that day Father said that he had decided to take a couple of the farm slaves and try to find out where Flavia's mother and brother might be. (Though privately I thought that they might both be dead.)

It was difficult for Father to know in which direction Flavia's home had been, since she had no clear idea of where she had been in those days of running from the Saxons.

However, when we asked whether there was any town near her home, she said that two days' journey away on horseback was the very city where Justin and Titus lived!

I was both excited and appalled at the thought of Saxon

war bands so close to them, but realized that they had the soldiers to defend them and of course The Wall!

I wanted to travel with Father, but he refused.

And so we women waited and waited for news…there are times when I wish I were a boy!

(I have to record that now I had Flavia to talk to, I was no longer lonely).

I try to understand how she must have felt being so completely alone.

It makes me think about Nessa, my bodyslave, who must have been taken away from her family too and our other slaves…do they wish to be free? Are they homesick for their own homes?

I have decided to make an effort always to be kind to Nessa and not treat the other slaves as though they were objects and not real people.

Talking of effort and remembering my resolve to be kinder to slaves I need to let Alexander have a rest from writing. Even he needs to have a break now and again!

Chapter 4

The Search for Flavia's Family

We, that is Mother, Flavia and I, had to wait for five days before Father returned exhausted. He had managed, more or less, to trace the route Flavia had taken. He and the two slaves had travelled eastwards, looking for any signs that the Saxons had passed that way and found themselves one evening deep in the forest which covered so much of the countryside around. As they were looking for a place where they could spread out their cloaks and sleep, the smell of cooking reached them. Cautiously, leaving their ponies tethered some way off, they walked on until, through the trees, they saw smoke rising. They realised that it was a Saxon settlement being built on the remains of a destroyed village. Although

it was dusk, Father said he thought he had seen one or two young boys among the workers who were hauling timber to make the round huts the Saxons built.

Flavia gave a cry of protest, quickly stifled, as my father looked very kindly at her. He asked' "Does your brother have dark hair?"

Flavia nodded and he continued, "It could be him then, but only you know him well enough to tell."

"I must go and see" said Flavia, "Can you send someone with me to show me the way?"

"Yes," my father's face was sad as he spoke, "But first we need to make a plan and decide whether there is any way we can get him away from the Saxons if it really *is* your brother."

I knew Flavia was desperate to know whether my father had found any trace of her mother and the baby, but couldn't bring herself to ask, so I asked instead.

"Father, did you see or hear anything of Flavia's mother and baby sister?"

Father hesitated and my mother gently put her arm around Flavia's shoulders as he replied,

"We met a woman hiding in the forest, who told us that she had seen a dark-haired woman carrying a bundle which could have been a baby, slowly stumbling along as if she was wounded. She tried to join her but the woman didn't seem to know what she was doing or where she was going. She had no obvious injury, but kept whispering piteously, 'My children, I must find them, I must find them.' They stayed together for the rest of that day and huddled together for warmth when it grew dark, but in the morning, the woman was gone."

Flavia buried her face in my mother's shoulder.

"Will I ever see them again?" she wept.

I remembered just then what the travelling preacher had said about God caring for the little things and found myself asking without words that God would take care of Flavia's family.

Father and Mother talked long into the evening that day

and I guess they were trying to decide what they could do to help, because the next morning, they called Flavia and myself into the atrium.

"We have been discussing when and how Flavia can go to try to rescue her brother and who should go with her", began my father, "It is not fitting that she should go alone with only a slave, Antonius, for company, so your mother has decided to accompany her. I wish that I could go also, but I cannot travel so far so soon again."

"What do you think, Julia?" asked mother, "Can you manage the household whilst I am gone?"

It was the first time my parents had asked for my opinion, but they did and I gave it!

"Mother," I said, as firmly as I could, "I should be the one to go with Flavia, not you; Father needs you and I have no skill in directing the whole household but I have had experience of danger and adventure!"

I knew they would be unhappy with what I had said, but I persisted in arguing how appropriate it would be if I went instead of Mother. It took a while, but eventually, Father said, "If I send Demetrius with you as well as Antonius, then I am willing to let you go, but I fear that so large a party of travellers will attract attention; you must be very careful."

We set off that day, with two ponies and rugs to wrap around us at night-time and plenty of barley bread and cheese and a few slightly withered apples from our orchard.

Our progress was slow as we kept a very careful watch for any Saxon bands on the forest tracks. We knew that some of them had rowed back to their own lands before the weather became too wintry, but some had stayed and settled down to begin a new life here on our richer lands.

It was on the third day early in the morning, that we smelt smoke and knew we were nearing the village.

My heart was pounding with a mixture of excitement and fear as we held a hurried council to determine what next we should do.

It was decided that Demetrius and Flavia should get as close to the village as possible while Antonius and I kept watch. (Our alarm signal would be the whistle of a blackbird repeated three times...Antonius is brilliant at mimicry!)

If they saw Paulinus, Flavia's brother, they would try to keep watch on his movements to see whether there might be a way of making contact with him.

That day, with us waiting in the cover of the trees, seemed endless! At last, we heard someone approaching. Antonius whistled and back came a very poor attempt at a blackbird's song, but at least we knew it was our friends!

Flavia was full of hope as she recounted the events of the day.

They had managed to get close to the village as the workers had set off for the forest and she was certain that one of the labourers was her brother. Some of the Saxons and their slaves felled trees and others cut them into useable lengths for building.

We spent a long time considering how to make contact with Paulinus, but until the workers in the clearing had gone back to the village when they'd finished their day's work, there was little we could do. Flavia thought she could ask Demetrius to carve a simple picture of an owl, whose call was their private signal call to each other, into the bark of a tree, and lay a pataran of sticks as an arrow pointing towards our hiding-place. I am sorry to say that it seemed to me to be a slim chance that her brother would notice any particular tree among all the others in the wood or any arrangements of sticks, but Flavia was so full of hope that I kept my thoughts to myself.

We returned to our ponies and waited for dusk. I don't think I have ever known such a long day!

We agreed that as soon as they thought it was safe, Flavia and Demetrius would slip away again as noiselessly as possible back to the clearing to find a suitable tree. We had no fears that the Saxons would understand the message even if they could speak a little of our language.

That night, I found it hard to sleep. The forest was full of noises I couldn't explain and I found myself wishing that Justin and even Titus were here with us. I remembered how we had kept one another's spirits up during the long hours of waiting for the Saxon assault on the city. How Justin's father Centurion Marcus had entrusted Justin with the safety of the family, giving him a sword to use if need be an how we had taken turns to climb the great wall that surrounded the city so we could see what was happening outside.

Eventually, in the coldest, darkest part of the night, I became aware of quiet stirrings beside me and heard the rustle of clothing as Flavia and Demetrius crept out of our sleeping-place. I had helped Flavia gather many sticks before we lay down, so all she had to do was find a good spot to set out her message.

The next thing I knew was Antonius shaking me awake.

"Move, quickly and quietly!" he urged, "Saxons coming this way!"

We gathered up our rugs and slipping from tree to tree, made our way to the ponies. At one point the group of Saxons passed so close that I felt sure they could have heard the hammering of my heart, but we reached the ponies without being spotted.

"What about Flavia and Demetrius?", I whispered, "do you think they'll be caught?" I wanted to run towards the village and try to warn them, but Antonius shook his head.

"Wait", he mouthed back at me, "just wait until we're sure the Saxons have gone. Then we'll give the signal and see if they answer."

It was horrible waiting there in the trees not knowing what was happening to our companions. I tried to breathe deeply to steady myself, closed my eyes and prayed and prayed that they would be kept safe.

Suddenly Antonius touched my arm, "They're coming!" he said quietly.

"Who's coming?" I asked hardly daring to hope.

"Our friends!" he said, and whistled the signal. The answer came back just as though a blackbird was calling.

Flavia and Demetrius arrived in the next moment and I hugged my friend tightly.

As we sat down to have our breakfast of bread, cheese and apples, they told us how they'd left a message near the spot where Paulinus had been working the day before. They planned to go back after work had finished for the day on the site to see if Paulinus had found the message and replied with one of his own.

That left a day in which to sleep a little and to consider ways of getting Paulinus away from the village. To be honest, it seemed to me very unlikely that he could make contact with us without his captors seeing and I think Demetrius and Antonius felt the same, but Flavia was still full of hope and so we kept our thoughts to ourselves.

Antonius suggested that we could try making a diversion and while attention was focussed away from the slaves, one of us could steal in and lead Paulinus out into the forest.

After a great deal of discussion it was decided that Antonius should circle round to the other side of the forest clearing and start a small fire, hoping that rain we had had recently was enough to stop any trees catching light. It was a desperate plan, but we couldn't see any other way of attracting attention, unless...

"What about taking one of the ponies with you and letting it go into the clearing?" suggested Flavia, "That should create enough of a diversion."

"Better if I ride it into the clearing!" said Demetrius, "and trust to the fact that the Saxons will be too surprised to hurl any knives at me!"

We were unhappy at his idea, but couldn't think of a better alternative.

(I forgot in my anxiety for Demetrius' safety that he was a slave and was therefore not considered as important as one of us Romans...all my concern was that he should not get hurt or captured himself. This reflection which surprised me considerably when I had time to think about it, I added myself later as Alexander might have been hurt by my reference to slaves. When I have more time, I must think about the whole idea of buying and selling people as slaves, although I know that my family's slaves are well cared for. Perhaps, though, they'd sooner be free and have to find their own food and clothes? Maybe I'll ask Nessa what she thinks when I have time to talk privately to her again.)

When it was dusk and the work in the clearing had

finished for the day, Flavia and Demetrius went back to see if Paulinus had left any reply to Flavia's stick message. To her joy, he had! His message was necessarily short...he had arranged the sticks into a word...it just said 'percipio' which meant he understood what Flavia had tried to show him.

Flavia took great care in rearranging the sticks to say 'wait for the pony, then run to us' Once she was sure all was right, she and Demetrius surveyed the clearing to find the best place for Demetrius to hide with the pony as soon as there was enough light to see but not be seen by any Saxons.

None of us slept much that night. It seemed endless! But at last, the darkness became less and a dim grey light filtered through the trees and Demetrius led his pony so silently away from our camping place that I was not aware that he had gone.

We gathered up the remains of food, hiding the sleeping rugs in a hollow made by the roots of a large oak tree so that the ponies were as lightly loaded as possible. Each remaining pony had to carry two people once we had rescued Paulinus and we knew we had to ride away as fast as we could.

Our walk to the hiding place we had chosen was as silent as we could make it, taking care not to tread on any sticks. It seemed a much longer way than I had remembered, but eventually we found the thicket of bushes which would give us shelter and stood to wait for the coming of the slaves.

My heart was thumping so hard, I was sure it could be heard by the others, but they were all concentrating on trying to stand still and not fidget, though Antonius gave me a huge wink as if he knew what I was feeling.

We were all taken by surprise when a few minutes after the slaves and their guards had arrived and the chains which joined them together had been undone, a pony thundered through the clearing, scattering slaves and Saxons, as they jumped out of the way.

Flavia was beckoning wildly to a boy who was staring around the clearing. Suddenly, he saw Flavia and charged towards us. Antonius grabbed him and hauled him onto his pony. Flavia and I scrambled onto ours and we set off at a breakneck speed away from the scene of chaos.

I think the surprise must have been so great that none of the Saxon guards had time to realise that one of their slaves was missing.

"Be careful of tree roots!" yelled Antonius, as we galloped among the overhanging trees towards a glimmer of light at the edge of the forest.

I do not know how none of us fell off or got thrown to the ground in that mad ride, but we all emerged from the trees and set off across more open country towards home, still so far away!

Our great anxiety now, was for Demetrius...had he got clear safely or had they managed to capture him?

When we stopped in the shelter of some trees to let the ponies rest, we discussed what we should do.

All of us were full of admiration for what Demetrius had done and I think more than one of us sent up a prayer to the God who cares for all, to keep Demetrius safe.

Antonius now took charge and made us keep moving away from the Saxon village even though he said we must walk a bit to ease the burden for the ponies.

At noon, we stopped for something to eat and were just getting ready to remount, when the sound of hooves hit our ears. A rider was approaching at a great pace.

A Saxon? Or could it be Demetrius?

"Get down and lie flat!" ordered Antonius, giving both ponies a gentle slap to move them away from us.

I was lying there with my face pressed into the rough grass, when I heard an amused laugh above me and a familiar voice panted, "What is this? Having a rest are we?"

"Demetrius!" I was so relieved to see him that I forgave him for laughing at me and jumped up to greet him with a huge smile.

Antonius came to say 'Well done' before we gathered the ponies and all set off at a more moderate pace on our homeward way.

It took another day and a half before we caught our first glimpse of the tiled roof and thatched barns of our farm. We were safe!

Chapter 5

Back in the City

I am resuming writing for a while...

Winter had come and almost gone before we set out for Titus' house; Flavia and Paulinus stayed at the farm with Father so they could rest and enjoy being together again.

As I said, it was good to see Justin and Olivia again and even Titus when he forgot to be noisy and argumentative.

I also enjoyed recounting my great adventure to Justin and Titus. I think they felt a little envious not to have been part of it!

We had spent a few days, as I wrote earlier, just doing the usual things: visits for me to Hermione and outings with Alexander and the boys down to the river. However, one day, Justin's mother asked if I would accompany her to the leather-worker's booth and help her with Olivia. She wanted to buy a gift for Justin as it was soon to be his birthday.

It was a bitterly cold day with an east wind whipping around all the corners between shops and sending swirls of dust across the market-place. As we crossed from the basilica towards the leather-worker's booth, I noticed a woman huddled in a tattered cloak trying to protect a child from the wind in the sparse shelter of a booth selling fish.

My mind went straightaway to what my father had told us of a dark-haired woman with a baby in the forest. Could it be Flavia's mother and sister?

I must have gasped because Justin's mother turned to look at me in surprise. I told her what I was thinking and she said very gently:

'Look after Olivia for me and I will go and speak with her.'

I watched her approach and bend down to say something. The woman looked up and I could see the streaks of dirt on her face and how thin she was.

A few moments later, Justin's mother came back leading the lady by the hand.

"This lady is Berenice. She escaped from Saxons who attacked her home and family a while ago."

My heart beat a little faster.

"Do you have a daughter called Flavia and a son, Paulinus?" I asked.

Imagine my excitement when her face lit up with an expression of wonder. She had no words, but simply nodded.

We could hardly wait to take her back to Justin's house where she was able to wash herself and the little girl. Justin's mother gave her a clean tunic and stola and some of Olivia's grown-out-of clothes for her daughter.

I ran round to fetch my mother from Titus' house and the three ladies sat for a long while chatting and crying a little too, before Centurion Marcus returned from duty and said he would arrange for Berenice to travel back to our farm and be reunited with her family.

Mother decided to cut short our visit to my aunt and return with them. Although I would have liked to go too and be part of the joyful reunion, I was quite pleased when Mother said that my aunt would be glad if I stayed on for a while. I knew also, that although I really liked Flavia, I would feel awkward and in the way while she and her family had some time together without too many other people there. They had a great deal to talk about and plans to make for the future. So, until Mother could resume her visit, I was glad to have more time with Titus and Justin.

Springtime had come with a rush and not only were there many swallows, but on the flat fields behind the shore, lambs were jumping and racing.

It was hard to consider dark things like raids and slavery when the world was so full of life and hope. When I stopped to think a little though, my heart was sad for all those slaves we had not been able to rescue and for all the people who had no one to look out for them.

One bright day when Alexander was feeling unwell and lessons were cancelled for the boys, they decided to go fishing down along the shore in the direction of the lagoon where the Saxons had moored their boats whilst waiting for the signal to attack the city when we had our great adventure. They had to ask permission to go outside the city walls of course and after some thought, Centurion Marcus agreed but said that he would ask one of the fishermen from the town to go with them who could take them along the shore in his boat.

Imagine my feelings when Justin came to my aunt's house to ask if I could go with them!

It seemed a long time before she made up her mind and I found I had been holding my breath while she deliberated...but at last she agreed as long as Nessa went with me. Titus began to object to having two girls in the boat with Justin and himself, but I stopped him by placing a hand firmly over his mouth which made Justin grin.

The morning was already getting towards noon when we finally set off on a flood tide out of the river and into the estuary. All afternoon the boys fished and Nessa and I sat trailing our hands in the water and watching the low mud banks slide past with a few birds poking around in the mud for food. Once we saw a hare lope across a meadow and both Nessa and I laughed as another hare jumped up and challenged the first hare to a boxing match...it was a moment of shared pleasure with someone I had thought of as inferior just a few weeks ago. Now I was having to rethink...how was Nessa inferior? Was it just that she belonged to a defeated people? That her parents were so poor that they had sold her into slavery? That she had not had my education and privileges? Was it in fact that we Romans with our superior army had become less by not showing mercy to the conquered ones...maybe they were the 'little' ones whom God cared for? A lot to ponder, but to get back to my account...(here Alexander takes over again and I feel a little ashamed of what I asked him to write about slaves earlier in the account. I think it's because I just forget that he isn't one of us. I wonder if I dare ask him why he is a slave and how he come to be one?)

CHAPTER 6

HIDDEN TREASURE

Our course along the estuary had now brought us very close to the place where the Saxon boats had anchored last year while they prepared to attack the city, (see Justin's account of our adventures then, which he called 'Fires in the Night'), and we were all feeling in need of food. Eunice, the cook in Justin's house had packed bread and cheese for us and some honey cakes, of course!

The fisherman whose name I don't know, brought the boat close into a small sandy, pebbly beach and helped us out. Needless to say, Titus managed to land in the water and splash everyone else in the process. However, once the fuss had died down we enjoyed our meal together and then Justin asked if the fisherman would tell us a local tale as we rested before setting off home again. We were very satisfied to sit back and listen, although his grasp of our language was not perfect.

This is the tale that he told us; a story of hidden treasure!

In the days when the Romans had not been in Britannia for many years, the tribe called the Iceni rose against the injustice done to their queen, Boudicca and her daughters after the death of her husband. They rode in war array to Camulodunum, Justin and Titus' city, and attacked it with the utmost ferocity- killing, burning and looting. There was little time for the citizens to find anywhere to escape to. In the panic, people either took their treasures with them as they ran, or hid them to be collected later when the terror had passed.

Sadly, most of the Romans who fled to the Temple of Claudius to be safe never returned home to collect their treasured possessions. The Iceni warriors set fire to the temple and all inside died.

One such family had been out in the fields when they saw the dust raised by the approaching army. They fled back to their home and while the mother gathered clothes and some food for the children, her husband ran to find a safe hiding place for their pieces of gold and silver and their jewellery. He hurriedly hid it, then joined his family as they ran to the temple, just reaching the great doors before the citizens closed and barricaded them. The story was told by a neighbour who managed to find safety by hiding in the hypocaust of his house, until the hordes had passed. This neighbour then fled to the countryside and it was many months before he felt it was safe to come back. When he did, he looked for the treasure without success. Soon afterwards he died and although the story spread widely when peace was restored and any one who had escaped the attack returned to the city, they were too busy rebuilding their homes and lives, to spend much time searching for treasure. To this day no one has ever found the precious items.

"So", said the fisherman, "there must be hidden treasure to be found in the city even now."

Much later, as we were walking back home from the river, I looked at the boys and felt that I knew they were thinking. How wonderful it would be to find some hidden treasure. I thought of Flavia and her family who had lost so much and knew that if we discovered any treasure, and sold it they might be able to find another home.

There was no opportunity to talk privately that evening, but the next day after lessons, I asked my aunt if I might go to Justin's house and play with Olivia. That was a little deceitful since I really wanted to talk to Justin, though I never mind spending time with Olivia and her doll which she calls her 'babba'.

I told Justin what I had in mind about looking for the lost treasure and helping Flavia and her family. He agreed that would be a good thing to do and we spent a happy hour suggesting various places we might try. I felt mean not involving Titus so when Justin asked if Titus knew what I wanted to do, I promised to tell him as soon as I saw him. I just hoped he wouldn't argue about helping Flavia's family!

Titus was surprisingly amenable to the suggestion that if we found any valuable objects we could sell at least some and help Flavia...(I really think he is growing up a bit at last).

A few days after that the three of us, having thought hard about where and how we could start our search, and failed to reach any agreement, called on Alexander to give us his advice. He thought hard for a few moments, then said, "After the burning of the city, the people who returned began to rebuild and as you know the wall was then erected as a defence so I think that anything to be found would have come to light then. I suggest that you make a note of anywhere not too far from the wall where there might be signs of older houses. Look for humpy pieces of ground", he added.

Titus gave a yell of excitement; "There are lots of humpy bits in our garden. Let's start looking there!"

Justin being more practical asked, "How will you convince your mother to let you dig up her garden?"

"Oh, she won't mind when I mention the word 'treasure'", said Titus, "anyway, she doesn't go down to the end where the humps are very often."

Alexander looked uneasy... "I think perhaps we shouldn't say anything about treasure to anyone else because if other people get to hear about it and they almost certainly will, who knows what might happen?"

He was being very tactful since we all knew how much my aunt loved to chat to her friends and acquaintances. I thought that if Titus told her, it wouldn't be long before all the street would have heard just a whisper, and then before much time had passed everyone would be speculating on the treasure hidden in Titus' family's garden, whether there really was any or not!

We agreed that one of us would dig under the humps while the others kept watch and of course Titus had to dig first. He soon got tired of turning up clods of soil and pieces of broken pots and handed over the spade to Justin, going indoors to clean his hands and get one of the slaves to wash the soil off his tunic.

I sat where I could see the house and Justin too but the sun was so warm that I began to feel very drowsy.

My eyes flew open as I realised my aunt was calling me. I ran to find her before she could come out and see Justin hard at work.

"Julia", she demanded as I panted into the atrium, "what is Titus doing with earth all over his clothes?"

"I think he's digging the garden....perhaps he's enjoying the fresh air." I knew my voice sounded very unconvincing and I wasn't surprised when aunt replied somewhat snappishly, "I can't imagine Titus would enjoy gardening for a moment...I just trust you are not finding mischief to get into like you did on your last visit!"

I noticed out of the corner of an eye that Alexander was crossing the atrium on the way to run an errand. I must have looked slightly desperate because he intervened to query my aunt about something, so allowing me to escape before she could start asking more awkward questions.

I ran back to where Justin was looking hot and fed up.

"There's nothing here but broken pots and dishes... how many pots can get broken in one house?" he asked in frustration.

"As many as the kitchen slaves drop or throw at each other in their arguments!" I giggled at the thought but Justin was not amused. He dropped the spade and said, "I'm going home to think a bit more...we're wasting time here."

The next few days were very rainy and none of us felt like digging in the wet so nothing was done and I knew that my time at my aunt's was soon coming to an end. I began to feel that we would never find any treasure before it was time for me to return home.

Then we had a day when the sun shone for a while and our hopes rose, only to be dashed when that evening there was a violent storm of wind and rain. It woke me up and I lay listening to the torrents of water streaming down outside and felt the shutters over the window being tugged by the wind. I felt quite frightened at the fierceness of the weather and said a prayer for protection before snuggling down to try to sleep again. However, by the morning, the storm had blown over and in the bright sunshine, raindrops on the wet grass sparkled like jewels. It seemed like a good sign that we should have another attempt to search for the treasure today. But the boys both had lessons, Justin's mother and Olivia were going to visit a friend and my aunt was occupied with getting a couple of slaves to go up on the roof and replace a broken tile which had caused a large puddle to appear in the triclinium where we had our meals.

I was free to do or go wherever I wanted since my aunt was too bothered to notice whether I was in the house or not, so I decided to go and see if I could find some flowers in the garden of the ruined temple along the road. I remembered seeing plants growing in abundance among the untended shrubs when we had made a den there last year and I thought it might cheer my aunt if I could find some spring flowers and make her a posy.

I slipped out of the house and walked quickly to the temple-site. Looking round to check that no-one was watching, I crept into into the overgrown garden at the back. My sandals very soon became sodden with rainwater so I took them off and hitched up my stola so it didn't get wet. I couldn't stop myself from gasping as I came around the corner of the ruins. Where the storm-rain had been so heavy, it had washed away a large section of soil from the base of the crumbling building and a large hole had opened up. It seemed to lead into the tunnels of a hypocaust. My heart was beating fast with excitement... how I wished I could explore inside the tunnels, but I was sensible enough to know that it was better not to venture inside on my own in case there was another landslip and I couldn't get out. No one would know where I was!

Any exploration would have to wait until Justin and Titus were able to come with me...perhaps later that afternoon?

I made myself stop wondering what we might find in the tunnels and started looking for flowers. I found some violets and a few daisies and twisted a piece of grass round the stems to make a pretty posy, then cautiously made my way out of the garden and back onto the street. Justin's mother and Olivia were just coming along and Olivia ran to greet me, waving her 'Babba'.

"Yuyu", (that's what she calls me), "come, play!"

I saw Justin's mother look at my soggy sandals and the dripping hem of my stola, but she didn't say anything and I walked back to their house with them.

When we were inside, she told me to take off my wet things and gave me one of her own stolas to wear. It was somewhat too large, but I didn't mind and the morning passed happily as Olivia and I dressed and undressed 'Babba' and enjoyed some of Eunice's honey-cakes.

By the time I needed to go back to my aunt's, my sandals and stola had been cleaned, and dried (more or less) by the warmth of Eunice's oven.

I think Aunt was pleased with her flowers (and she *hadn't* noticed I had been gone for hours!).

As soon as I could, I told Titus what I had found in the temple garden. He insisted we go straight away to find Justin so that the three of us could go and explore the tunnels, but Justin was going out with his father to buy a dagger that he had been promised for his birthday. After Titus had been persuaded by me (with a great deal of tactfulness) that he and I should wait until Justin could join us, he came back home with me, grumbling loudly.

However, the next day the weather was warm and sunny, so after lessons Justin joined Titus and myself in the grounds of the ruined temple and I showed the boys the great hole in the ground under the temple. It was agreed that two should creep into the tunnels and explore while the other one kept watch outside. You can guess who had to stay outside!

I listened to the boys' voices as they crawled away into the darkness, until I could no longer hear them. A thrush was singing among the tangled bushes and the sun was so warm on my face, that in that moment I felt totally content. Suddenly, a shout came from somewhere inside the tunnel.

I ran over to the hole and peered in. Titus appeared crawling backwards, followed by Justin. Titus was yelling something which I couldn't hear until he emerged dirty and excited from the hole, waving a leather bag.

"The treasure!" he shouted.

I looked at Justin who had now dragged himself out into the open air. He too looked pleased.

"Is it?" I asked him.

He nodded, "I think it might be, but", he took the bag from Titus, "I think we should let you open it since you couldn't come with us."

He really is a nice, thoughtful boy!

I held the bag in my hands. It felt light, but there was something inside.

Carefully, with Titus breathing heavily down my neck, I pulled undone the strings that were tied around it and gently opened out the leather pouch. As I did so, the strings crumbled in my hand and the neck of the bag fell open almost spilling out what was inside. The cracked and dirty leather held something that showed glints of gold in the sunshine as I carefully held it up. It was a necklace strung with garnets There was also a silver bracelet, some gold earrings and two rings set with amethyst stones. The last item was a golden spoon such as a baby might have used. They were all tarnished, but we were sure they were very valuable.

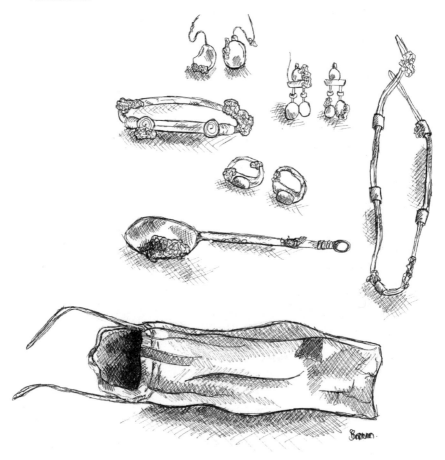

For once, Titus was awed into silence, but Justin said, "The family this belonged to must have lived close by here. I suppose they thought this little temple would be a safe place to hide their treasure, since maybe Boudicca's warriors would respect a sacred space and not destroy it."

I gazed at the treasures, wondering about the family who had run for their lives, leaving it behind to collect once the danger was past. All at once, a great feeling of sorrow came over me as I thought how they had never come back but had died in the fires Boudicca had lit to burn and destroy the city. A tear ran down my cheek and I was quite glad when Titus took the pouch out of my hands to look at the items more closely. Justin came over to me and put his arm round my shoulder, giving it a gentle squeeze.

"Think of how much good we can do with this," he said, "I'm sure the family these belonged to would be glad they were used to help another family in need."

He was right, of course, but I still felt sad for that unknown family, especially for the baby.

We sat on the wall in the temple grounds for a while discussing how we could sell the treasures to help Flavia's family. In the end we decided to ask Justin's father to take charge of it for us. The next problem was how to get Justin and Titus back into their houses without anyone seeing the dirty state of their clothes.

I offered to make a diversion by calling at Justin's home to see Olivia and talking to his Mother while he slipped into his sleeping cell and changed his tunic. I wasn't bothered about Titus since he could talk his way out of any trouble at home!

Later that day Justin, Titus and I met to discuss how we

should go about telling our families of our find. We agreed that Centurion Marcus was the best person to show the treasure to them, so once we had told him what we had found, he helped us to explain to the rest of our families how and where we had found it, (though we hurried over the bit where the two boys had crawled through the hypocaust tunnels, since we felt it would worry the mothers unnecessarily!). Alexander was of the opinion that it was probably buried under the floor of the nearest building to the family's house which being a temple would not attract much attention from the raiders. The ruins of the family home were probably covered over when the Wall was built years later.

We knew that once everyone in my aunt's house had seen the treasure it would be very hard to keep the news from spreading around the neighbourhood! Sure enough, it wasn't very many days before people began to find an excuse to visit my aunt or Justin's family and ask to see the treasure. Justin's father looked for a safe place to keep it until he found a possible buyer for the jewellery. One of the other centurions at the fortress had a merchant friend who was eager to see the objects and I was amazed at how anxious we had become to get rid of it before it attracted the attention of a thief.

One night, I woke suddenly. As I lay there, I was sure I heard something outside my window, which faced onto the street. The shutters didn't quite meet in the middle so I crept out of bed and padded over to the window. Very cautiously, I peeped through the gap. What I saw made my heart race. A hand was feeling along the shutter towards the gap. It was a moment of horror...what should I do?

Scream? Run and wake Alexander? I was afraid that if I left my sleeping cell, the owner of the hand would be able to force the shutter apart before I could get help. As I considered my options, I remembered that earlier in the day, I had found an unusually-shaped piece of wood in the garden and brought it into the house for Alexander to carve into a little animal for Olivia...(wood-carving is yet another of that amazing Alexander's talents!). The wood was beside my bed so as quickly and as quietly as I could, I tiptoed across the room and picked it up. Back at the window, I waited until the hand had reached the place where the shutters didn't meet, then using all my strength, hit it very hard. There was a muffled cry, the hand disappeared and there was the sound of running footsteps. Sadly, I had also broken one of the shutters and made a considerable amount of noise. A light appeared in the corridor outside my sleeping cell and voices exclaimed loudly, my aunt's one of the loudest among them.

After the shock of what I had done I found it hard to move but I managed to open my door and try to reassure my aunt that all was now well. Alexander helped to calm things down and settle the household again. He also took time to fix more wood over the broken shutters. I found I was shivering now that the danger was over and I think Alexander must have understood because he spoke very kindly to me, fetched me a lamp and a warm drink and and offered to bring his mattress and sleep outside my room if I was still afraid.

In the morning we told Centurion Marcus what had happened and he frowned, saying, "The sooner I can sell the treasure, the better".

Eventually, his fellow centurion told him, that the merchant trading in jewellery was in the city for a few days on his travels and would like to see the objects very soon.

The price Justin's father got for the treasure was astounding and I knew it would not only provide for a new start for Berenice and her family, but would give us enough money to buy a few nice things. (We had kept the child's spoon for Flavia's little sister and decided that Berenice should have the largest share and the rest would be divided equally among our three families..)

As I held the coins which were my share, I thought again about the family who had perished so long ago. It seemed for a moment that time had somehow slipped and I could feel their panic and see the father frantically burying their treasures under the earth floor of the temple, not knowing that he would never return to rescue it and that years later, a protective wall would be built on the ruins of their home. I wondered what I would do if my family had faced the same danger so suddenly with no time to prepare. I imagined my father burying these objects I held in my hand and my mother's jewels as a horde of enemies approached. Perhaps the Saxons would come one day and we would have to do just that...would someone in the future dig up *our* treasure?

CHAPTER 7

As I said, we had not sold the child's spoon to the merchant and I looked forward to presenting it to Berenice for the little one to use.

Although I was pleased to enjoy spending time with my friends in the city, I was also eager to get home and give the money we had from the treasure to Flavia's family. What a difference it would make to them who had so very little!

Later that evening I sat writing on the bench under the damson tree for a long time:

As I thought about it, I realised how much I had taken for granted. My life was so comfortable compared to many people's.

I suddenly found myself thinking of Nessa. All that she had was what we gave her. The only thing that was her own was a small bracelet which she said her mother had given her. I realised that I knew nothing about Nessa's family, not even why she had become a slave or whether her mother was alive or dead. I had always assumed that her parents had to sell her after some trouble. This made me feel quite ashamed...I had just accepted her as my possession; to fetch things for me, to bring me drinks or food whenever I felt in need of a snack, to wash and style my hair and help me dress. How could I have so rarely considered her feelings? Again, I resolved to be more thoughtful towards Nessa when I was at home once more. I could not imagine that my own mother and father would ever sell me.

That night the air was very warm, so I got up and crept quietly further down the long garden where the inevitable noises from the house were muted and looked up at the sky. A large, full moon was rising, gilding the roof top with silvery light. I suddenly wanted to see Justin and share the beauty of the moonlit garden with him. The intensity of my feeling took me by surprise; I must spend some time thinking about it...perhaps I am wanting Justin to be more than just a friend? Could I be falling in love?

(You will see that I have to write this myself. It is far too private even for Alexander to see.)

Before I could explore this most interesting question further, my aunt called from the house:

"Julia, Centurion Marcus is here to see you."

I was surprised. Why would Justin's father want to see me?

"Julia, I need to ask a favour of you," he began, "Olivia is feverish and my wife is feeling unwell too. She needs to sleep so if

54

your aunt is willing would you come and look after Olivia for a few hours until I return from duty?"

I walked with him the short way to their house, then he left to go to his duty and I greeted Justin's mother quietly and went to keep watch over Olivia.

Justin came to sit with me and we talked in whispers so as not to wake her.

I cannot remember what we spoke of,...anything and nothing probably.

I felt so helpless and found myself praying: 'Oh, please! Oh please!'

Justin's mother reappeared, looking tired and sad.

"Olivia," she whispered, "Wake up".

The little girl opened her eyes, sighed once, then shut them again.

"Will she recover?"

I didn't realise I had spoken out loud, but Justin's mother looked at me with a brave attempt at a smile and said, "If we cool her down enough so the fever goes, she will have a chance of recovery, but I don't know. We will let you know in the morning. Thank you for your help. You should go back home now. Justin will accompany you."

The moon was still bright, but I hardly noticed it as we walked back to my aunt's house not talking. As we came to the entrance, I turned to Justin and reached out my hand.

"I'm so sorry Justin..." I could say no more for tears. He took

my hand without speaking and gripped it tightly, then turned away to go home.

I found it hard to sleep. After tossing and turning for a long time, I got out of bed and tugged open the shutters over the window. The moon was well down in the sky and somehow its brightness now seemed cold and uncaring. I started to cry. Was there really a Father who cared that Olivia lay so ill? She was surely one of the 'little ones' that Brother Lukas had talked about. As I stood there, my thoughts whirling, I cried out into the night sky;

"If you are really there, Great Father, please take care of Olivia!"

Suddenly I felt as if the lightest of touches had brushed my face and an unexpected peace wrapped itself around me.

I crept back to bed and slept until Nessa woke me with a message from Justin. Olivia was a little better.

Oh how glad I was! I couldn't bear to think of her no longer with us, not hearing her little voice calling,'Yuyu' any more or seeing the look of concentration on her face as she dressed or undressed her 'Baba'.

A few days later, I was on my way home happy to know that although she was pale and a little listless, Olivia was going to be well again. She had even managed a smile when I went round to say 'goodbye' and toddled out to wave as I left.

It was hard to leave my friends not knowing when I would see them again.

(This next bit I'm writing later at home.)

When I had said my farewells to Justin's family, he accompanied me back to my aunt's house.

"I will miss you, Julia", he said. Taking my hand, he kissed it and gave me a small gift.

"Open it when you are at home and remember me". He smiled at me but spoke solemnly.

During the journey back my mind was full of wonder. Sometimes I felt like a bird, flying high among the clouds, then my heart sank as the distance between us increased.

I knew that soon Justin and Titus would be given their white togas as a sign of entering the adult world and that my parents would be looking for a suitable husband for me.

A sadness swept over me as I realised that childhood was rapidly being left behind and perhaps there would be no more adventures.

As it happened, I was wrong!

CHAPTER 8

And this is what happened quite unexpectedly one day as autumn again turned leaves in our forests golden and the blackberries were ripening on the bushes.

It had been a busy time since I had returned home, helping Berenice and her family find a new home. There was a small villa not far from our farm which had once been a flourishing farm itself, but the couple who lived there were now old and the husband had fallen sick. They had had to sell their slaves and the land had been left to nature.

Father approached the two old people on Berenice's behalf and offered them a good price for their villa and the land. They were reluctant to leave their home having no family to live with, so it was agreed that Berenice would have two rooms added to the villa and let them stay there. It turned out to be the best arrangement!

Berenice had company who had much wisdom about how to run the farm, little Helena had ready-made grandparents and child-minders and Flavia and Paulinus enjoyed hearing stories of life when all was peaceful and prosperous.

To help the family start cultivating the land, Father sent Anthonius to help them with the heavy work of ploughing fields and planting fruit trees. He had been gone for several weeks and his hard work and commonsense was sorely missed here. I know Father would have liked to command his return, but was reluctant to deprive Berenice of his help. Anyway, he and Demetrius did as best as they could without him, in fact we had all helped gathering the harvest in.

Because Flavia now lived so close, I was able to go and visit her. It was about an hour's walk and I enjoyed the exercise whenever mother would allow me to go. I usually took Nessa for company and one of the large hounds that Father had bought as guards after the happenings of last year.

A year had passed and summer was fading into Autumn again. One particularly fine day when the breeze felt warm on our faces and I was not required for anything special since Mother had a friend with her, I asked permission to go to see Flavia.

It was such a beautiful day that I felt the urge to explore and when I had greeted Flavia and her family, I suggested that if she could be spared, we go up onto the low, chalky hills that surround her new home and walk along the ancient trackway that crowned the ridge for a long way before dropping down to lower ground.

It was so old that no one knew who has first made it and as we walked among the whispering trees that had grown up beside the track finding some ripe blackberries, it felt as though if I looked round I might see one of those ancient people among the bushes. So you can imagine my shock when the dog growled and bounded towards a clump of young thorn trees. A face peered out from behind the trees, I heard a stifled shout of alarm and then the sounds of a scuffle as the dog attacked.

Flavia was trembling beside me and my own heart was beating fast as I ran towards the sounds, yelling to the dog at the same time.

I rounded the clump of trees and saw a young man, dirty and dishevelled, backed up against a tree trunk while Dog kept guard, growling all the while.

I stared at the lad. He was not merely mud-spattered but had a great tear in the side of his tunic which was stained with blood. It was obvious he was wounded and even as I stood there, he seemed to crumple and subsided onto the ground in a tangled heap. Flavia, who had crept up to join me, trembled again and whispered,

"A Saxon, it's a Saxon". She gave a frightened whimper and added, "Suppose there are others...I'm scared, Julia...let's go quickly!"

She tugged at my cloak and when I didn't move, pulled harder... "Julia, please!!"

"Flavia", I said, giving her a little shake, "run back the way we came and find Anthonius or one of the farm workers and bring them here."

"But what about you?" she was whimpering again.

"Just go!" My voice must have sounded authoritative, because giving me one scared look, she ran off.

"And hurry!" I added, quite unnecessarily, since she fled like a frightened rabbit along the old track.

For a while I stood watching the lad with questions whirling around in my mind.

Was he a Saxon? Apart from his fair hair, he could almost have been one of us Romans. I guessed that Justin was a similar height and possibly much the same age. We had been so frightened of the Saxons for as long as I could remember, so why wasn't I more scared of him?

I felt ashamed when I recalled half-thinking that Saxons had horns growing out of their heads as well as on their helmets and would be armed with axes, daggers, swords and clubs.

But now, how could I be afraid of someone who looked so ordinary?

I knelt down beside the lad, who had not moved, wondering if he was actually dead, but when I reached out and touched his skinny arm, he stirred.

"Who are you?" I asked him. He opened his eyes and gave another groan, then shut them again. I repeated my question but it was clear he didn't understand what I was asking.

It seemed a very long time before Flavia reappeared, panting heavily, with Anthonius and a farm hand.

"Are you all right?" Anthonius gave me a searching look, but when I nodded, he gave his attention to the boy on the ground.

"Can we do anything for him?" I asked.

Anthonius exchanged a glance with Servius, the farmhand, they took hold of the boy and lifted him carefully between them.

"We'll take him back to the farm", said Anthonius, "clean him up and see how bad his injuries are. Then we can decide what to do next."

They tried not to jolt their burden, but inevitably he was shaken a little on the journey back along the rough track and each time, he moaned in pain. Once, his eyes fluttered open and I realised with a shock that they were as blue as the pale Autumn sky. Most of my Roman family and friends were dark-eyed and olive-skinned, though some had grey eyes and fair skin.

Back at Flavia's home, Berenice found salves and bandages while Anthonius and Servius stripped the boy and washed his wounds. He had lost much blood from a deep gash in his side and appeared to have some broken ribs.

Once this was done, they found clean clothing for him and left him to sleep on a sleeping mat which Berenice found for him.

Flavia and I spent much time discussing the events of the day. Flavia was full of admiration for me for having stayed with the Saxon. As she talked, I found that I could understand her fears; after all, I had not seen a Saxon war band in action nor been captured by one.

I very much wished I could talk over all that had happened with Justin, but it would be a long time before I saw him again. The thought of him made my heart warm and to Flavia's astonishment I found myself smiling.

When the time came for me to return home, the Saxon lad had recovered consciousness and I was eager to know more about him.

Sensing my desire, Berenice very kindly invited me to come again soon, but it was several days before Mother could spare me again.

When I returned to Flavia's home, the Saxon was sitting up though still very weak.

"Servius can understand a little of the Saxon's language and has found out his name is Aethelred and he was injured in a skirmish," Flavia told me.

"But," I said, "why was he wandering here and alone?"

We went to find Servius and asked him if he had found out

anything more. He told us that as far as he could make out, the warband of which Aethelred was a part had met with strong resistance and abandoned their attempt to seize a prosperous villa many miles from here. Because of his injuries, Aethelred had been left behind when they fled and though faint from loss of blood, had managed to find enough strength to stumble along not knowing where he was going.

I thought he must have been very strong to have come so far.

"Where will he go now?" I asked Servius.

"Nowhere! At least not yet." It was Anthonius who answered thoughtfully.

I was very surprised that Berenice had given shelter, even welcomed to her home, someone who belonged to the people who had killed her husband and destroyed her home.

One day, when Flavia had some task to do outside and Helena had just gone for her afternoon sleep, I asked Berenice what had made her accept Aethelred as willingly as she did.

"I follow the teachings of the Christus, 'The Way'", she answered, "and He taught us to forgive and show kindness to all."

"Even your enemies who did so much wrong to you?" I said incredulously.

"Yes." she said, "As He forgave those who killed Him".

Her answer made me feel uncomfortable as I thought of the way I had felt and spoken about our enemies in the past.

I could not help asking, "Are you not afraid that others will come looking for him and burn your home again?"

"Sometimes", Berenice admitted, "I am very afraid, but I remember that I can trust God, the Great Father, with my life and family."

That made me recall how I myself had asked the Great Father for protection. I felt that I would like to know more about 'The Way', but we were interrupted by a wail from Helena and the moment passed.

I visited the family several times in the weeks that followed and each time I saw him Aethelred had grown stronger and had begun to learn our language a little. In return, Flavia and I would hold up a stone or a leaf and tell him the Roman word and Aethelred would then repeat it and tell us what it was in his language. We had great fun trying to get our tongues around the Saxon words which he taught us and often we would laugh until we nearly cried. Aethelred began to laugh with us and something of the sadness which had enveloped him fell away.

As the weeks passed and the weather became colder, it seemed as though Aethelred had become part of Berenice's family and she would not hear of his leaving until the Spring.

Now I am back in the city and so have no news of how things are on Berenice's farm.

And...Alexander is scribing for me again for which I am most grateful!!

CHAPTER 9

Spring has come again and Mother and I are paying another visit to my aunt. Justin has grown tall and slim, Titus is still chubby but taller than me which is a little disconcerting! He is also still very noisy and argumentative. Olivia can say my name properly now and runs everywhere, still carrying her 'babba' with her. Alexander is in the process of making her a small wheeled carriage for 'babba' about which she is very excited.

Justin and Titus are both at grammarium, learning skills which will enable them to take part in politics and debate when they are officially adults. I feel that Titus has quite a lot to learn about reasoned debate!

However, after the day's lessons, we spend time together. Sometimes we walk down to the river and watch the boats loading and unloading at the quay. There are always many different languages to be heard and merchants from far away countries buying and selling. I wondered whether the merchant who bought our treasure was among them and where he had sold it.

One day as we were returning home from the river we saw smoke billowing up from a narrow street. One of the houses was alight and judging by the shouts and screams, someone was trapped inside.

A crowd of people was surging towards the scene and we found ourselves caught up among them. Titus fought his way through the crowd to see what was happening. Justin made to follow him, then turned back and took my hand.

"I need to get you home, Julia," he said, "I don't think we can do anything here to help."

As we made our way out of the crowd, Titus panted up behind us.

"All is well," he puffed, "the screaming was because the woman who owned the house had lost everything in the fire."

"But", he added, looking at me, "everyone was safe."

We found out later from Centurion Marcus that the woman had bought a few valuable items from a merchant who had lodged with her whenever he came to the city and after the flames had died away, there was no trace of them. All that remained was the shell of the building.

I exchanged a glance with Justin we were both thinking the same thing. It was *our* treasure that had been lost, or at least, some of it.

"Perhaps it wasn't meant to belong to anyone except the family who first owned it," I said and shivered.

Titus grinned, "Perhaps it had a curse on it!"

I turned my back on him... "I don't believe in such things", I said crossly and left the boys to stare after me with amazement.

I knew that many people believed in curses, but it just felt wrong to imagine that the treasure we had found that had belonged to a family probably just like ours could have made anything so bad happen. It seemed to me that it was people that made trouble not lifeless things like jewellery.

Justin pointed out to me when we discussed the matter later, that actually even if the things themselves didn't cause disaster, many people would fight and steal to possess them so that in a way they did make bad things happen.

We found out a few days afterwards that it was the same merchant to whom Justin's father had sold our treasure that had stayed in the burned-out house.

He had not returned from buying and selling in the north of Britannia and with the house gone no one knew whather he had left anything behind or not.

I thought that maybe he had left any objects he didn't want to carry on a long journey and hidden them somewhere about the now-ruined house but we would never know unless he came back and as far as I know he never did.

The rest of the visit to my aunt was pleasant. I was very happy in Justin's company and I think he felt the same, but it would be years before he was deemed ready to marry and I knew my parents had someone in mind for me.

One day when the sun was bright, the blue of the sky suddenly reminded me of Aethelred. I wondered how he was faring. Would he go to find a band of his countrymen and join them?

I began to feel it was time to go home and catch up again with events there though I knew it would be hard to part with Justin.

Chapter 10

Mother was ready too to return to our villa and Father, so soon afterwards we set off on the journey home.

Writing later:

I had said farewell to Titus and Justin the evening before as they would be at lessons when we left. As before, Justin gave me a small gift and seeing the tears in my eyes, he leant forward and gently kissed my hand.

"I wish..." he began. His voice tailed off and he stopped.

"Yes?" I prompted. But he just kissed my hand again and said, "Write to me." Then he was gone and my heart felt very heavy.

Mother looked at me very kindly when I joined her in the travelling carriage.

I waited until we were once again at home before opening the gift. It was a ring set with a piece of amber; something I had admired when we were in the market one day.

It was on my finger when I next visited Flavia's family. Aethelred was out in the fields with Anthonius when I arrived, but when he came in for the midday meal, I noticed that he kept looking at it.

Finally he asked, "Where did you get the ring?"

To my surprise, he was speaking our language well. He added that amber was found on the sea shore in the country he'd come from and was very popular with Saxon people.

I explained that the ring had come from a trader in the market, in the city who must have travelled in Aethelred's country.

"Do you think this trader might have news of my people?" Aethelred's voice was husky.

It was clear that he wanted to know what was happening among his own countrymen, but nothing more was said until Flavia and I were sitting in the sunshine later on. Then Flavia turned to me with an expression on her face that was hard to read;

"Do you think Aethelred will leave us now to find his own folk?"

I pondered for a moment then said, "Will you be sad if he does?"

Flavia's cheeks coloured and she murmured, "Perhaps", adding, "I know he will be missed on the farm. Now he has recovered, he works very hard."

I smiled to myself then sighed, thinking of Justin. So far, Father had not said anything of my marriage and I dared to hope that he might be willing to allow me to stay at home until...until what? Until Justin had finished his education and was deemed old enough to take a wife? Maybe his father would want him to marry into a well-to-do family in the city.

I realised that as I was the only child of my parents, I had a privileged position in that I truly think Father sometimes forgot I was a girl and allowed me freedoms that normally only a son would have. I suppose that in some respects Anthonius was like a son to him and would probably inherit the farm when Father died.

I gave myself a mental shake and tried to think about something else.

Aethelred appeared at that moment with a message for Flavia from her mother, so I had the opportunity to talk to him on my own. He hesitated and then asked

"You have friends in the city, Julia, don't you? Do you think they might know where I might find my kinsmen?"

70

Before I could stop myself, I blurted out, "Why do you want to find the people who abandoned you when you have a good home here with Berenice and Flavia? Don't you think you owe them something for their kindness to you?"

He didn't answer but gave me a long look, then turned away.

But I think that he did take some notice of what I said, because there was no more talk of leaving and he seemed to settle as the hard work of getting the harvest in began.

At the end of those weeks of harvesting, both on Berenice's farm and ours we held a feast to celebrate.

There was dancing and singing with dishes of rabbit caught in the fields, cooked with onions, blackberries and damsons stewed with honey from Anthonius' hives and loaves of barley bread made by Flavia and myself with much laughter as we danced around trying to get the sticky dough off our hands.

At the end of the evening as the huge harvest moon was sailing up above the chalky fields, Anthonius and Berenice made a startling announcement. They had decided (with Father's blessing of course as the head of our household) to marry. That meant that we would lose Anthonius from our household and I knew Father would find that very hard.

Flavia was understandably very excited and pleased that her mother to had found happiness again but the next time I saw her she was distraught.

"Aethelred has gone!", She flung herself down on the sofa in the triclinium. Her hair was in disarray and her face streaked with tears.

Truth to tell, I was not as surprised as I might have been. I had noticed of late that he often had a far away look in those blue eyes of his as though he was already on his way to his own people.

"Did he leave a message?" I enquired.

"He told Anthonius to tell me that he needed to go to quiet his heart, but he would return when he had seen his family again. But when that will be, if ever, he didn't say."

I thought maybe Flavia needed to be in a different place for a while, so I asked Berenice if she could spare her daughter to visit me at home for a few days.

Flavia seemed happy to come, but she was still moping around after several days with us, so one morning, while we were sitting in the atrium of our house, sewing some new cushions, I said what was on my mind.

"Flavia, how can you be in love with someone who belongs to the people who killed your father, captured you and your brother and has left the farm without saying goodbye or thanking you and your mother for your kindness?!"

She looked at me with tears in her eyes and replied,

"He is so strong but hates violence. He only came with the war band because he wanted an adventure, but all the killing sickened him. You just don't understand, Julia".

Yes, I do, I thought grimly, thinking of the pain I endured feeling for someone who was so far away from me in every way.

I swallowed my annoyance and suggested that we go for a walk even though the wind was strong, blowing leaves off trees and setting them dancing on the paving stones outside.

In spite of herself, Flavia joined me as we ran, blown like the leaves by the wind along the track above the farm where I had first met her. It was so wild that we couldn't help laughing as we held on to each other and by the time we returned, she was much brighter, especially when we saw Demetrius trying to sweep the leaves up in vain as they were scattered again straight away.

That night I felt I must speak to Father about my future and try to explain what I felt for Justin.

I am so glad I did, because just two days later, he collapsed out in the fields and died in Demetrius' arms as Demetrius carried him back to the house.

It was an unbelievably sad time for mother and me. Flavia felt she should go home to tell Anthonius and he was soon with us, giving what help and support he could.

Although I had not spent much time with him, I felt numb at the loss of this man who had cared for his household quietly and well, though so often in pain.

I relived our last real conversation when I had asked about his plans for me.

"Julia," he had said, "I have someone in mind for you, but most of all I want you to be happy and I am in no hurry to lose you. I think your mother needs you more than you realise."

He hadn't told me who his intended bridegroom was for me

though I thought Mother would know. But I didn't want to find out yet, my heart was still like a dead weight inside me.

Father was buried with a simple ceremony, Anthonius returned to his new wife and family and Mother and I tried to carry on as usual, but I know that sometimes Mother wept in secret.

It was at this time that Brother Lukas came visiting again and Mother invited him to spend some days staying with us and teaching. As before, friends and people from all around, including Anthonius, Berenice and their household, gathered to hear him as he told us more of what the Christus had said and done. I was very much occupied helping Mother and the house slaves prepare and serve refreshment for them all, but I still heard some of what he said and wished I could hear more. It was on the last evening of his visit that Brother Lukas came to me and said,

"Child, I see that you are sad. Take comfort from the One who gave us His peace and whose love can heal every broken heart if it will open to Him."

I pondered his words when I was alone that night. If only I could let my heart open but it felt so heavy and closed.

If it hadn't been for Demetrius and his cheerful service, I think both Mother and I would have sunk into depression that winter. It was very cold. Mist and snow blanketed the fields and hills for weeks. Even the clouds seemed to emphasise our feeling of loss and gloom and when the thaw came, it felt as though we had been mourning for ever. But as the water began to trickle and gurgle again in the streams, I felt a small flame of hope rise and when Gwyn arrived in the atrium one day purring loudly with a swagger, I was interested enough to investigate the cause of his self-satisfaction. He ate the food Demetrius had prepared for him, then strolled outside again, heading for one of the barns.

To my delight, there in the straw was a small tortoiseshell cat licking three beautiful kittens; one was the same colour as its mother, one was white with patches of brown and black but one was pure white.

"Oh, Gwyn, you clever boy!" I exclaimed as I knelt down to pick up a kitten and hold it close to me. Suddenly, tears came and I crouched there in the straw weeping until Nessa came to find me and ran for Mother.

Mother held me close and we cried together until it felt as though all the sadness of the last few months was washed away.

A few days later a message came from my aunt inviting us to come and stay as long as we liked now the weather was better.

It was a welcome invitation and we soon set out for Camulodunum leaving Demetrius in charge at home.

CHAPTER 11

Once again Alexander is my faithful scribe!

Although the days are still chilly, there are times when I'm sure I can detect scents of earth and growing things on the air, though Titus scoffs at my fancies. I don't know why I bother to share anything with that boy! He is very cross at present because his mother refuses to let him learn to drive a chariot. I think she fears that he would drive far too fast, upset the chariot and be killed, a thing which seems more than likely to me!

It is particularly hard because having taught Justin to handle a chariot, Centurion Marcus takes him to the circus to practise racing with the fast little chariot ponies. Titus is very jealous.But although I don't say so, I very much hope we will be able to watch Justin race in a competition soon.

The chance to do so came sooner than I had thought!

After weeks of lessons and practice, Centurion Marcus was at last satisfied that Justin was capable of handling a team of racing ponies and he was allowed to race in the next games.

Titus grumpily said he wasn't interested but I suspected he wouldn't want to stay at home alone when we were all planning to go and watch!

Sure enough on the morning of the race, when Centurion Marcus, Justin's mother and a very excited Olivia came to walk with us to the circus, Titus appeared and joined us all. Olivia skipped along holding my hand, chatting excitedly about seeing the ponies racing;

"Fast, fast" she said, "Justin make them go fast!"

It was very noisy as we took our seats on the benches in the stands either side of the track. I wondered whether Justin was feeling as nervous as I was!

The race began and I saw with amusement that Titus was jumping up and down shouting for Justin at the top of his voice...(a not inconsiderable noise!)

We ladies did not shout, but I noticed Justin's mother clasping her hands tightly and I was holding Olivia so firmly that she squirmed in protest.

"Juliaaaa!"

"Sorry, little one", I let go of her and she wriggled free, squeaking, "Justin, fast, faster!"

Inwardly I was yelling with her, willing Justin to overtake his rival as he swept round the curve at the far end of the course. There was one breath-stopping moment when the two chariots were so close that the wheel hubs hit each other and a collision seemed inevitable, but Justin managed to steer away before his chariot turned over though it lurched

sickeningly. My hands flew up to cover my mouth and I felt slightly sick.

The manoevre to avoid the other chariot had lost Justin time and as the ponies raced to the finish line, he was just behind his rival who waved triumphantly as he crossed the line. The crowd cheered both drivers loudly.

I was so proud of Justin and I think his parents were too. He climbed down from his perch and patted the sweating ponies before they were led away by a groom. Centurion Marcus walked over to his son and embraced him with an arm round his shoulders.

"Well done, son.", he said "You handled that chariot very well, especially when the other driver hit you!"

Later, when we were back at my aunt's house, I went out into the garden and thought about Justin. As if I had conjured him up by the intensity of my feelings, Justin appeared, looking weary but content. Titus followed him out so I knew there wouldn't be much opportunity to talk to him.

"Julia," he began, "thank you for coming to watch today".

"I wouldn't have missed it." I said, "It was very exciting!"

He smiled at me and my heart flipped.

Titus looked at us and grinned, but before he could make any comment, Alexander came to fetch him for something his mother wanted him to do.

Justin and I sat on the bench under the damson tree in a friendly silence.

"What will you and your mother do now?" he asked, "Will you stay at the farm or move here to live near your aunt?"

"I really don't know", I replied, "Mother hasn't told me what Father's plans were for my marriage and I haven't asked her, because..." my voice tailed away.

"I think," I continued, "that if I were not there, Mother would hand the farm over to Anthonius as Father's heir and come to live with my aunt, but it would be very hard for her. Perhaps I should not marry, but stay with her."

"If you could wait", he began, stopping as Titus returned, with Alexander carrying a dish of honey cakes and the moment was lost. I could have wept!

CHAPTER 12

It was only a few days after that when some devastating news came. The soldiers were all being recalled to help defend Rome from the Germanic tribes who had been attacking the Empire for many years, but were now threatening to destroy it.

Centurion Marcus had gathered his family together and told them that he would have to leave within a very short time.

"I will have to go ahead of you with my troops, but when the time seems right, I will send for you to join me." His face was very sad as he spoke, looking round at his precious family.

Although Justin knew the time would come when the family had to face change, he found it very hard to accept that their life in Britannia was coming to an end. He had never lived anywhere else.

He came to tell me the dreadful news. Titus was out at his wrestling class and we were alone.

"*This* is my country," he declared passionately, "I know Father must do his duty, but what has Rome to do with us? I have no desire to fight for somewhere I don't know."

He told me that he had spoken with his father of his hope to become an architect and builder rather than a soldier even though he was expected to follow Centurion Marcus into the Eagles, the Roman Army.

My heart was heavy as I looked at the tenseness in his face and thought of the dangers that faced Centurion Marcus and his family. How would little Olivia would cope with such disruption? How would I cope with not seeing Justin ever again?

We stared miserably at each other, then Justin broke the silence.

"I feel like doing something mad," he began, "What about climbing the wall again?"

"Oh, yes!" I said, "Now, before my aunt and mother want me for something."

So we set off straight away to the garden of the ruined temple where we had found the treasure. I hitched up my toga not caring that it was unladylike and scrambled up with Justin's help until we could sit unseen on the top of the wall.

"How long ago it seems since we were last up here, when we were watching the flight of the traitor from the city to join the Saxons." My face must have shown something of what I was thinking because Justin agreed, 'We were so much younger then and so frightened of the Saxons!'

'And now,' I added, 'Flavia is in love with one!'

Justin gave me a quizzical look, 'Is she? After all they did to her and her family?'

He stared out across the countryside to the distant horizon. Smoke from many cooking fires drifted up among the trees and he looked as though he was remembering the night up on the wall, when he had seen the fires of burning homesteads and farms.

'Perhaps one day, all this country will be a mixture of people, Romans, Saxons, the tribes and nobody will think of the others as their enemies.'

I thought privately that was unlikely. It seemed to me that people would always look at others who were different from them with suspicion, would always want more than they had and fight to get it. However I said nothing to Justin. Perhaps his faith would be justified and Britannia would be peaceful in spite of the withdrawal of the Roman soldiers.

We sat on the wall lost in our thoughts for a long while until I heard my name being shouted from below.

'We'd better go', I said reluctantly. 'Oh, Justin' I added, 'Please! If you must go, come back again!'

He smiled rather sadly and replied, 'Julia, if I can, I will. This is where I will always belong.'

So we slipped and scrambled back down off the wall that had seen the beginning of Justin's adventures and would probably still be there when we were grown up and who knows where we might be by then!

CHARACTERS

On the Farm:

Julia: She is thirteen years old, nearly fourteen, tall and slim, of determined character. She lives with her parents on a farm in the west of what is now called Essex.

Aquila: Julia's father, retired from the 'Eagles' the Roman Army with injuries received in battle. He is often in pain but likes to spend time in the open air, cultivating the land given to him after his retirement.

Drusilla: Julia's mother is a very capable woman who helps her husband with the farm and manages the household with a firm hand. She likes to visit her widowed sister in the city as often as she can.

Prisca: Drusilla's body slave.

Nessa: She was sold by her parents to be Julia's special slave when they lost their home and land in a rebellion against the Romans.

Demetrius: He is a trusted member of the household slaves, brought back to Britannia when he saved Aquila's life in a skirmish. He was offered his freedom by Aquila but chose to remain with the family, although he is regarded as more of a friend than a slave.

Anthonius: A soldier in the 'Eagles', he was a member of Aquila's century until invalided out of the army with a damaged leg. When Aquila was wounded, he looked after him, having lost any family of his own to raiders. With no one to belong to and nowhere to go, Aquila gave him position in his household as farm-worker and handyman. He is very skilled at mending things.

In the City:

Justin: Justin is growing into manhood. Soon he will be old enough to become an adult, taking off the 'bulla' or golden charm which has hung round his neck since childhood and changing his bordered toga for a pure white one which signifies his 'coming of age'. He attends the 'grammarium' at the forum in the city, has lessons still with Alexander and learns military skills from his father.

Marcus: A centurion at the garrison, the father of Justin and Olivia. He is a firm, but kind-hearted head of the family and is highly-regarded in the city as an honest and fair man.

Priscilla: Justin's mother. She is also kind-hearted and understanding. She is very fond of her two children and looks after her household well and wisely with thought for others.

Olivia: She is Justin's sister born quite a long time after Justin. She is an engaging child with a merry little face and Justin is very fond of her.

Claudia: Julia's aunt. She has been widowed for a long time and has very little control over her only, and spoilt, son Titus.

Alexander: Born and educated in Greece, he was sold into slavery as a young man. He is intelligent and learned and has been tutor to Justin and Titus for several years.

Titus: Julia's cousin. His father is dead and he is rather spoiled by his mother and grandmother. He is noisy and, unlike Justin, not given to reflection before he opens his mouth or embarks on a course of action.

Hermione: She is a friend of Julia's and lives in the same city as Justin and Titus where her father commands the Roman garrison.

Other Characters:

Flavia: Julia meets her unexpectedly on the hillside above the farm as she escapes from Saxon raiders who killed her father and captured her brother, Paulinus. In the confusion as the raiders set fire to her home, she loses contact with her mother and her baby siser. Disorientated and afraid, she flees from the scene and becomes lost.

Berenice: Flavia's mother who fought bravely to try and save her husband and home was also captured but by a different Saxon band from Paulinus. She manages to get away after a few days, but not knowing where her children are. She also flees but in a different direction from Flavia.

Paulinus: Flavia's brother, taken as a slave by the chief of one of the two Saxon raiding parties, is chained and set to work with others to build a new Saxon settlement in the forest which covers much of that part of the country.

Helena: Flavia's baby sister

Servius: A farm worker employed by Anthonius to help on Berenice's farm

Aethelred: A Saxon who was encountered by Flavia and Julia near the farm.

Brother Lukas: a travelling monk who visited Julia's home more than once.

FAMILY LIFE IN ROMAN BRITAIN

Here is a little information about Roman families which explains some of the things in the story that seem strange to us.

The life of a Roman family was in some respects very different from ours although the people were similar in their feelings to us in many ways.

As the 'Paterfamilias' or head of the family, Centurion Marcus and Julia's father would take all the major decisions for their families. So Julia's father would choose whom she was to marry and as he had no male heir, he chose to treat Anthonius as his son and heir.

Nessa's family were so poor that they chose to sell her as a slave rather than starve. This may seem dreadful to us, but at least she was well-fed and given clothes and a bed to sleep in.

Sheila Lloyd MA: writer and teacher

4th century AD: A tale of young people living in Roman Britain. We're intrigued to learn how different their way of life was, their clothes, their food, their homes.... We're delighted to discover how like us they were, the fears and hopes they had, the risks they took, the trouble they got into... And we're glad to find that they shared similar values of acceptance, compassion and forgiveness.

Adventure, danger, rescue; friendship, kindness and hospitality, all add up to a really good read.

Isaac N. Sixth-former

I really like the language the most as it allows me to imagine the world very clearly.

Dr P. Ditchburn BA (Hons).MA. PhD

Here at last we have the second book following on from 'Fires in the Night' continuing the particular adventures of Justin, Titus and Julia. The story is set in 4th century Roman Britain when the culture of slavery was very much part of life, as indeed was Social Status.

This is a glimpse into life in Britain under Roman rule, and the impact of the Saxon response. We follow the coming of age of Julia as she grows into a young woman, and questions the accepted norms of society around her, including slavery during this period, which will hopefully stir the imaginations of the young readers, and encourage them to seek more information about the history of Britain.

As in all good books for young people there are several interwoven adventures, including marauding Saxons and hidden treasure, making this a gripping tale and a must read, especially for young people learning about Roman Britain.

Anna aged 11

I loved learning about the history and the adventure. I enjoyed the mystery; wondering what's going to happen next.

Hope it's not too long until there's a new book in the series.

Anna Giles, mother of teenagers

Told with warmth and compassion, Mary's story is a joy to read, transporting us to life in Roman Britain through the young heroine's diary. Mary weaves together pacey adventures with the ups and downs of daily life from schooling to clothing and home-cooking – I, for one, am keen to try Eunice's honey cakes!

Imaginations will be sparked by the treasure-hunting trio. Who wouldn't love to find a hoard in their local area?

When life circumstances have the potential to change very suddenly, Mary combines loss and grief with love, hope and yearning and we glimpse signs of maturity in the young people and their thoughtful consideration of others.

I can't wait for the next instalment.

Orlagh 13 years

Dear Mary, I have read your book and it is a great book. I really liked it.

THANKS AND ACKNOWLEDGEMENTS

I would like to thank the people who have been in any way involved in the writing of this sequel to 'Fires in the Night'. I cannot name them all here, but would mention Philip Crummy who gave me the idea of including the Fenwick Treasure and Paul at Aspect Print who has taken pains to give the book its final shape.

My especial thanks go to 20-year-old Sophie who has drawn the pictures for the story...her first attempt at book illustration! She has patiently tried to incorporate my suggestions and I am so pleased with what she has produced.

Thanks as always to my family and friends for their kind support and encouragement, especially grandchildren who took the time to read and comment on the story.

As I wrote in my last book, I am still on the journey of faith in God, Whose care and forgiveness, Julia begins to understand and appreciate as she meets other followers of The Way.